# MATT AND DAVE

# YUCK

## YUCK'S FART CLUB
## CLUB
### AND
## YUCK'S SICK TRICK

**Illustrated by Nigel Baines**

www.yuckweb.com

**FOR FARTERS:**

Toby  You  Maya

Ava  Pete  Lyla

Inez  Guy

SIMON AND SCHUSTER

First published in Great Britain in 2006
by Simon & Schuster UK Ltd
**A CBS COMPANY**

Africa House 64-78 Kingsway London WC2B 6AH

3 5 7 9 10 8 6 4 2

A CIP catalogue record for this book is
available from the British Library

ISBN 1-416-91092-1
EAN 9781416910923

Typeset by Nigel Baines
Printed and bound in Great Britain by
Cox & Wyman Ltd, Reading, Berkshire

www.simonsays.co.uk

# There was a boy so disgusting they called him Yuck

# YUCK'S
# FART
# CLUB

Polly Princess sniffed.

Mum sniffed.

Dad sniffed.

"Who's farted?" Mum asked.

"It wasn't me," Polly said. "I never fart."

"It wasn't me," Dad said. "I almost
never fart."

"Well, it certainly wasn't me," Mum said.

Mum, Dad and Polly looked at Yuck.

Yuck scooped a spoonful of beans into his mouth.

"What?" he said.

"No farting, Yuck," Mum told him.
Yuck chewed his beans.

**PARP!**

Tomato sauce dribbled down his chin.

**BRRAAMP!**

"Perhaps you shouldn't have any more beans, Yuck," Dad said.

Yuck scooped another spoonful of beans into his mouth.

He shifted in his seat.

**RRRRRRiiiiiPPPPP!**

"Yuck!" everyone yelled. "That's disgusting!"

Really DISGUSTING!

MORE FART GAS

Polly covered her nose and mouth with her hands.

"Right, Yuck! That's enough beans for you!" Mum said, grabbing his plate.

"But I like beans."

Yuck decided that when he was EMPEROR OF EVERYTHING, he would have a swimming pool full of beans. Every morning he would dive into it, swimming and eating and farting, farting and eating and swimming.

"No more farting!" Mum said.

But Yuck had other ideas…

That afternoon his friends were coming round to play.

Polly Princess stood outside Yuck's bedroom door spying through the keyhole.

Yuck, Fartin Martin, Tom Bum and Little Eric were sitting in a circle around a big metal box.

Polly opened the door.

"What are you doing?" she asked.

"Mind your own business."

"What's in that box?"

"Go away, Polly," Yuck said.

"Not until you tell me what's in the box."

"It's a secret. This is a secret club. Go away." And Yuck sat on the box so she couldn't open it.

"It won't be a secret for long," Polly said.

She turned and stomped out of the room.

Yuck waited until he heard Polly's bedroom door click shut, then he gave the signal, picked up the big metal box and crept downstairs. Fartin Martin, Tom Bum and Little Eric followed him through the kitchen and out the back door.

Polly watched from her bedroom window as Yuck and his friends ran down the garden to the treehouse. They climbed up the rope ladder and hurried inside.

Yuck was carrying the big metal box.

He leaned out of the treehouse, pulled the rope ladder up so no one could follow them, then closed the rickety door.

Polly went to fetch Dad's binoculars.

Inside the treehouse, Yuck, Fartin Martin, Tom Bum and Little Eric sat around the big metal box.

"Is everyone ready?" Yuck asked.

Everyone nodded.

A spider scurried across the floor.

"Then welcome to Fart Club," Yuck said.

He lifted the lid on the big metal box and a golden-orange glow lit up the treehouse. The box was filled to the brim with cold,

wet, glistening beans.

Fartin Martin dipped his hand in.

"Not so fast," Yuck said. "First we've all got to swear by the rules."

"What rules?" Fartin Martin asked.

Yuck lowered his voice.

"Show me some skin," he said.

He held out his hand.

Fartin Martin, Tom Bum and Little Eric placed their hands on top of Yuck's.

"The first rule of Fart Club is – you don't talk about Fart Club," Yuck said.

Everyone nodded.

Yuck continued. "The second rule of Fart Club is – there are no more rules! You can fart whenever and however you want. All agree?"

"We swear on our farts," everyone said.

"Then let Fart Club begin."

Yuck dipped his hand in the box, right up to his elbow, and scooped out a handful

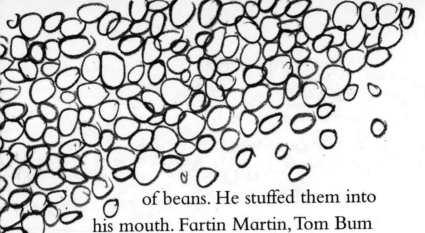

of beans. He stuffed them into his mouth. Fartin Martin, Tom Bum and Little Eric did the same. They chomped and slurped, chewed and swallowed, handful after handful of beans.

Then they sat back and waited.

"In Fart Club, you can grunt, guff, trump, pop, blow, whiz and let off as much as you like," Yuck said. "Just make sure it's big, loud and smelly."

Fartin Martin nodded.

Tom Bum nodded.

Little Eric nodded.

Yuck farted.

**PARP!**

Everyone sniffed. "Phwoarrr! What a STINKER!"

Fartin Martin farted.

His bottom jumped up and down on the wooden planks.

"I felt that," Little Eric said.

"A BOUNCER!" Yuck said.

Tom Bum lifted his leg in the air and let out a long one.

Little Eric coughed.

Fartin Martin pinched his nose.

"A GAS PIPE!" Yuck said. "Brilliant!"

"Thanks," Tom Bum replied. He lowered his leg to turn off the gas.

Everyone looked at Little Eric.

Little Eric scrunched his face. He was squeezing.

"I'm trying," he said.

He held his breath and pushed. His face turned red as he squeezed and strained and...

"Done it!"

"What?" Tom Bum asked.

"My fart," Little Eric said.

"I didn't hear anything."

"Nor me," Yuck said.

Then they all sniffed.

"Phwoarrr!"

"SILENT BUT VIOLENT," Little Eric said.

**PARP!** went Yuck.

**THRU BADU BADU BADU BA!**
went Fartin Martin.

**HiSSSSSSSSSSSSSSSSSS!**
went Tom Bum.

**━━━━━!** went Little Eric.

They did HONKERS and POPPERS, BLASTERS and SNEAKERS, CRACKERS and SQUIDGERS, but most of all… really smelly STINKERS!

And the more they farted the more they laughed. And the more they laughed the more they farted!

The treehouse slowly filled with gas until they were sitting in a thick smelly cloud.

"What's going on up there?"

Yuck peered through a crack between the wooden planks. It was Polly.

"Skids," he swore.

Polly was walking towards the tree.

"Quick – start the fans!" Yuck said.

Fartin Martin, Tom Bum and Little Eric flapped their arms, trying to get rid of the smell.

Yuck opened the rickety door to let in the breeze.

"What are you doing up there?" Polly cried. She was standing at the bottom of the tree.

"Nothing," Yuck said.

"Well Mum says dinner's ready, it's time to come in. Drop the ladder down – now!"

"Just coming."

Yuck ducked back inside the treehouse and closed the lid on the big metal box.

"Fart Club will meet again the same time next week," he said. "And everyone bring something with them. We're going to turn up the gas."

He waited for the air to clear, then dropped the rope ladder to the ground.

Fartin Martin, Tom Bum and Little Eric climbed down. Yuck came after them, carrying the big metal box under his arm.

"What were you doing up there?" Polly asked.

"Nothing," Yuck said.

"What's in the box?"

"Nothing," Yuck said.

"I don't believe you!"

"I already told you, Polly, it's a secret."

Yuck, Fartin Martin, Tom Bum and Little Eric walked back up the garden in silence.

And all the next week, none of them talked about Fart Club. But they were ALL thinking about it, ALL the time: what new smells they could make, what new sounds they could make, and who could do the biggest.

Yuck practised at night – farting under his duvet.

Fartin Martin practised in the bath —
making bubbles.

Tom Bum practised in his garage —
filling his bike tyres with fart gas.

And Little Eric practised in the library –
letting off silently.

The following Saturday, Polly Princess
watched through the binoculars from her
bedroom window. With her was Juicy Lucy,
Little Eric's sister.

"Why are we spying on them?" Juicy
Lucy asked.

"Because they're up to something," Polly

whispered. "They're going to the treehouse!"

"Let me see!" Lucy said.

Polly handed her the binoculars.

Yuck, Fartin Martin, Tom Bum and Little Eric ran down the garden and climbed the rope ladder to the treehouse.

"Yuck's carrying a big metal box," Lucy said.

"I told you!" Polly replied, grabbing the binoculars back.

"What's in it?" Lucy asked.

"I don't know," Polly said. "But we're going to find out."

She watched as the rope ladder went up and the door of the treehouse slammed shut.

Inside, everyone sat around the big metal box.

"Is everyone ready?" Yuck asked.

Everyone nodded.

Woodlice scurried up the walls.

"Then let Fart Club begin!"

cough splutter must... reach (cough) air

Yuck lifted the lid on the big metal box and the treehouse filled with a golden-orange glow.

Handful by handful, they gobbled the beans, sat back and...

"Did you all bring something?" Yuck asked.

Everyone nodded.

Fartin Martin went first.

He lifted his cap. Underneath, nesting in his hair, was a hard-boiled egg.

"I call this THE FUNKY CHICKEN," he said.

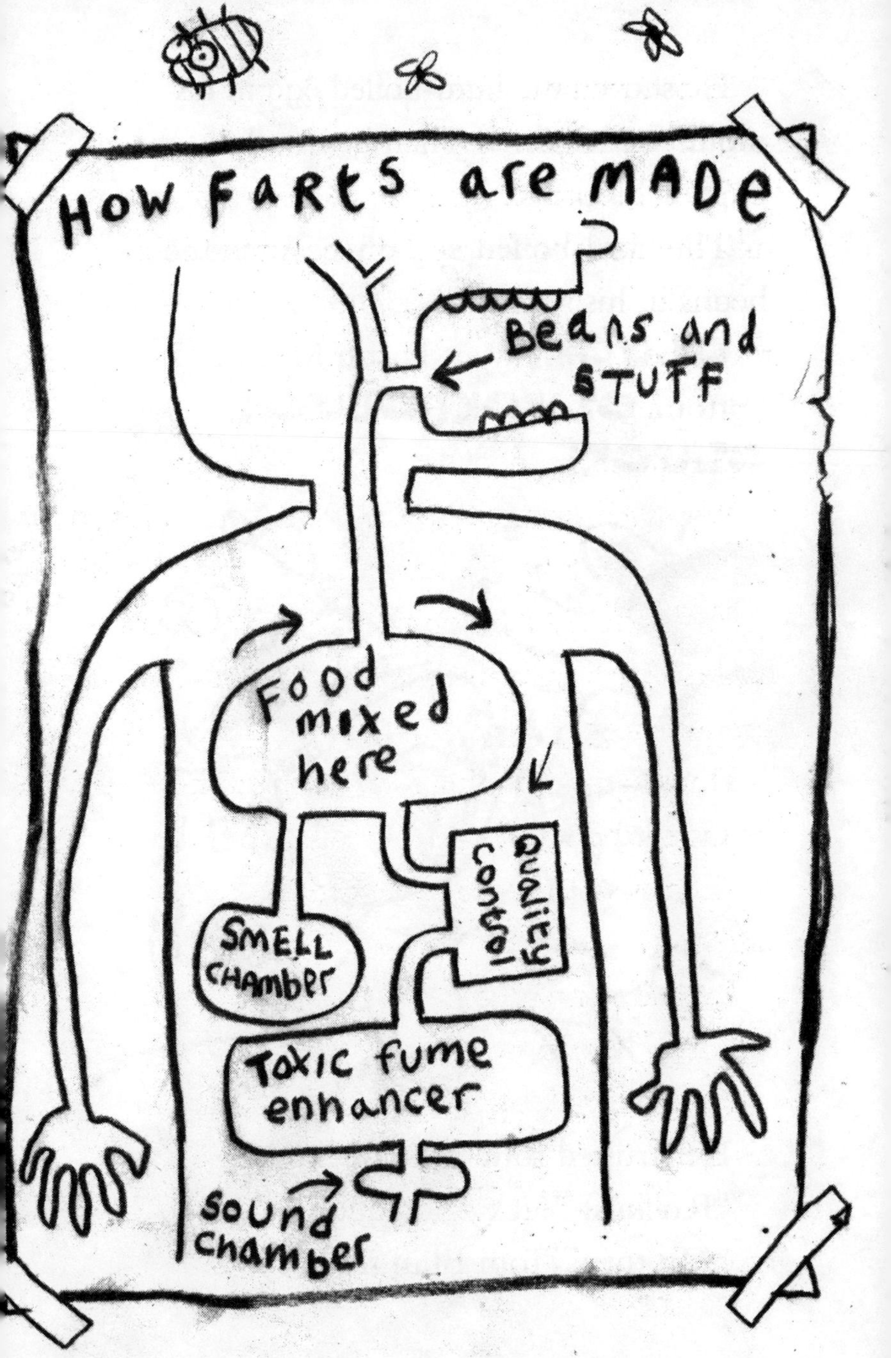

How FARTS are MADE

Beans and STUFF

Food mixed here

Quality Control

SMELL CHAMBER

Toxic fume enhancer

Sound chamber

He shoved the hard-boiled egg in his mouth and chewed. Then he stood up and flapped his arms.

The hard-boiled egg mixed with the beans in his stomach.

**CLUCK!** went Fartin Martin's bottom. **CLUCK! CLUCK! CLUCK!**

He strutted round the treehouse.

"Rockits!" Yuck said, laughing.

"My turn!" Tom Bum said.

From his pocket Tom Bum took out half
a hot dog.

"I call this THE DIRTY DOG," he said.

He bit into the hot dog and knelt down
on all fours. The beans and the hot dog
rumbled in his stomach.

**WOOF!** went Tom Bum's bottom.
**WOOF! WOOF!**

"Let me have a go," Little Eric said.

He pulled out a whole cabbage. It was as
big as his head.

"Are you going to eat all that?"

"I call it THE DEAD RAT," he told them.

Yuck, Fartin Martin and Tom Bum stared
at the cabbage.

"What's a dead rat got to do with a cabbage?" Tom Bum asked.

"You wait till you smell it," Little Eric said.

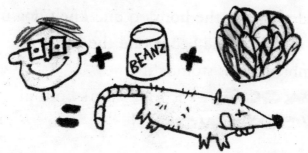

He munched the cabbage and scrunched his face.

The cabbage mixed with the beans.

Little Eric squeezed...

——— !

A fart sneaked out silently.

"PHWOARRR!"

Yuck, Fartin Martin and Tom Bum pulled their T-shirts over their faces.

"Good, isn't it?" Little Eric said.

Everyone coughed. "Dead rats!"

They waited for the smell to die down, then Yuck opened a can of Coola Cola.

He glugged it down in one.

There was a rumbling sound from Yuck's stomach as the Coola Cola mixed with the beans.

"I call this THE BUBBLER," Yuck said.

He lay on his back with his knees up.

He let out a little burp, then his bottom let out a little burp too. Cola-coloured gas started leaking from Yuck's shorts. It expanded to form a bubble that slowly rose into the air. Yuck pushed and another bubble burped out, then another. They floated around the treehouse.

Fartin Martin, Tom Bum and Little Eric reached out and popped the bubbles with their fingers.

**PARP!** went each bubble as it burst.

Meanwhile, Polly Princess and Juicy Lucy were hiding in the bushes at the bottom of the garden.

"What do you think they're doing in there?" Lucy asked.

"I thought I heard a dog," Polly said.

"I thought I heard a chicken," Lucy said. She peered through the binoculars. "The door's closed. I can't see anything."

"Let's sneak up on them."

"But they've pulled the rope ladder up."

Polly glared at Lucy. "I want to see what's in that box!" She looked at the tree.

"If I stand on your shoulders I could reach a branch and peek through the cracks in the floor of the treehouse."

"But what if they catch us?"

"Keep really quiet!"

Inside the treehouse, Fartin Martin was waving a sardine. "I call this one THE SLIPPERY FISH," he said.

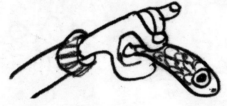

He gobbled the sardine in one, then lay on his front.

There was a squelching sound as the fish mixed with the beans.

He let out a big wet one.

FLiPiLLOPOLiPiLLOPOL

He shivered and wriggled.

A fart was flapping around in his pants, trying to escape.

"Are you all right?" Little Eric asked.

"It feels brilliant!" Fartin Martin said, wriggling.

Tom Bum pulled out a bag of popcorn. He opened it and started scoffing.

"I invented this in the cinema," he said, spraying popcorn everywhere. "It's called THE EXHAUST PIPE."

The popcorn mixed with the beans in Tom Bum's stomach. He squatted, pretending he was holding the steering wheel of a car.

"Awesome!" Fartin Martin said. His pants were still flapping.

"How about this then?" Little Eric said. In his hand he held a raw onion.

"Are you sure?" Yuck asked.

Little Eric raised the onion to his mouth and bit into it. He winced and took another bite. And another.

The onion mixed with the beans.

He squeezed.

Gas crept silently along the floor and up the walls.

Everyone sniffed and their eyes started to water.

"It's called THE STINGER," Little Eric said.

Yuck rubbed his eyes.

Fartin Martin rubbed his eyes.

Tom Bum rubbed his eyes.

Little Eric wiped away a tear.

"I'm so happy," he said.

"You haven't seen anything yet," Yuck told them. "Watch this!"

Yuck was holding a can of spaghetti.

"Spaghetti doesn't make you fart," Fartin Martin said.

"This is alphabetti spaghetti!"

Yuck opened the can, dipped his finger in and swirled the spaghetti letters in their tomato sauce.

He picked out an H, an E, two Ls and an O, then swallowed them.

He let out the gas. The fart said...

Yuck picked out some more letters, swallowed them and...

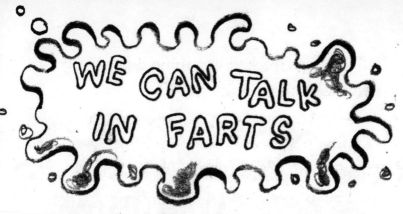

WE CAN TALK IN FARTS

"TALKING FARTS! Can I have a go?"
Little Eric said, sniffing.

"And me!" Fartin Martin said.

"And me!" Tom Bum said.

Yuck, Fartin Martin, Tom Bum and Little
Eric lay on their backs with their legs in
the air.

Tom Bum picked out some letters,
swallowed them and...

I'VE GOT A JOKE. WHAT DID THE BURP SAY TO THE FART?

Little Eric picked out some letters, swallowed them and...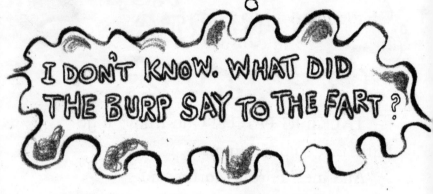

Tom Bum picked out some letters, swallowed them and...

Outside, Polly and Lucy looked up at the treehouse.

"Are you ready?" Polly whispered.

Lucy nodded.

"Then let's do it."

Lucy knelt down and Polly climbed onto
her shoulders.

Little Eric looked through a crack in the
floor. He picked out some more letters,
swallowed them and...

He pointed downwards.

Yuck, Fartin Martin and Tom Bum
looked through the cracks in the floor.

Fartin Martin dipped into the alphabetti
spaghetti. He grabbed a handful of letters,
swallowed them and...

Yuck looked around the treehouse. He
spied something scuttling up the wall.
Swallowing some letters he farted...

Polly was standing on Lucy's shoulders.

"Can you see?" Lucy whispered.

"Hold me steady," Polly said.

"Hurry up." Lucy was clutching Polly's
ankles. "I can't hold you much longer."

"I'm nearly there." Polly stretched for the
branch. "Just a little bit further."

But as her fingertips touched the branch,
she felt something hairy drop onto her face.

"Uuurrrggghhh!" she cried.

"Stay still," Lucy said.

Polly looked up and saw Yuck sitting in
the door of the treehouse. He dangled a
spider above her.

"Don't you dare,
Yuck!" she screeched.

Yuck let go.

The spider dropped.

"EEEEKKKK!" Polly
screamed as it fell into
her hair.

Then Yuck dropped
a caterpillar.

It landed on her nose.

"AAAGGGHHH!"

"Stop wobbling!"
Lucy said. "You're going
to fall."

But just then Yuck
dropped a centipede
and a handful of
woodlice. They
showered down on Polly
and Lucy.

"Get them off me!
Get them off me!" they
both cried.

Polly wobbled. Lucy wobbled.

"I hate you, Yuck!" Polly cried as she tumbled to the ground.

"Ouch!" Lucy said, crumpling beneath her.

Above them, the rope ladder lowered. Yuck, Fartin Martin, Tom Bum and Little Eric climbed down. They were laughing.

"Looks like we've caught a couple of spies," Yuck said. The big metal box was tucked safely under his arm.

"You wait!" Polly Princess told him. "I'll find out what you're up to! And what's in that stupid box!"

"Me too!" Juicy Lucy said.

But Yuck was already walking back to the house.

Little Eric followed behind him. "Fart Club ROCKS!" he said.

"Shhhh, remember the rules," Yuck whispered. "Don't talk about You-Know-What. Next week we'll go for the world's biggest fart!"

And over the following days, no one said a word. But they did leave each other messages....

SATURDAY AFTER LUNCH THE TREEHOUSE THE WORLD'S BIGGEST FART!

And the next Saturday they met again.

Polly and Lucy watched as Yuck, Fartin Martin, Tom Bum and Little Eric ran down the garden to the treehouse.

Polly had a plan.

Yuck pulled the rope ladder up and closed the door of the treehouse.

They sat around the big metal box.

"Is everyone ready?"

Everyone nodded.

All the insects in the treehouse ran for cover.

"Then let Fart Club begin!"

Yuck lifted the lid on the big metal box and the treehouse filled with a golden-orange glow. Handful by handful, they gobbled the beans and...

Fartin Martin, Tom Bum and Little Eric gasped.

At the bottom of the box was a hard-boiled egg, half a hot dog, a whole cabbage, a can of Coola Cola, a sardine, a bag of popcorn, a raw onion and a can of alphabetti spaghetti.

"The world's biggest fart will need it ALL."

"All at the same time?" Tom Bum asked.

"ALL of it!"

"That'll cause an explosion!" Fartin Martin said.

"It's called THE ROOM CLEARER," Yuck told them. "The biggest, loudest, smelliest fart in the whole wide world."

"Sounds d-d-d-dangerous to me," Little Eric said.

"You don't have to do it if you don't want to," Yuck told him.

Little Eric shook his head.

Tom Bum shook his head.

Fartin Martin shook his head.

"You do it, Yuck," they said.

Yuck took a deep breath.

Fartin Martin, Tom Bum and Little Eric watched as Yuck shoved the hard-boiled egg in his mouth and chewed. He bit into the hot dog. He munched the cabbage. He glugged the Coola Cola in one. He gobbled the sardine. He scoffed the popcorn. He bit into the raw onion. He winced and took another bite. And another. He swallowed every letter from the alphabetti spaghetti.

BACK INSIDE YUCK'S STOMACH

When he had finished, he lay on the
floor of the treehouse holding his legs in the
air. Everyone waited.

Polly Princess and Juicy Lucy were in
Dad's tool shed.

"I've got a plan," Polly whispered. "We'll
use Dad's ladder! We'll climb up and catch
them."

"And get the box!" Lucy said.

"I'll dash in, grab the box and throw it
down to you. We'll be in and out before
they know it."

Polly and Lucy took Dad's ladder
from the tool shed.

"Are you OK, Yuck?" Fartin Martin asked.

"You've gone a bit funny-looking," Tom Bum said.

"Your legs are trembling," Little Eric said.

"Stand back," Yuck told them.

Something bumped against the side of the treehouse.

"What was that?"

Fartin Martin peered through a gap in the wall. "It's Polly and Lucy! They've got a ladder!"

"Get out!" Yuck said. "I'm going to blow!"

"But you'll get caught!" Little Eric said.

"It's too late!" Yuck's stomach was rumbling.

It grew louder...

And LOUDER...

"Get out! Run!" he said.

Tom Bum flung open the door and threw the rope ladder down.

"Run for your lives!"

Fartin Martin, Tom Bum and Little Eric raced down the rope ladder.

As they went down they passed

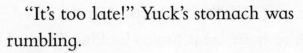

Polly on Dad's ladder.

She was going up!

"Where are you lot going?" Polly asked.

"Run!" Little Eric said.

"What's going on? Where's Yuck?"

Fartin Martin, Tom Bum and Little Eric
dived for cover in the bushes.

Polly climbed higher.

Then all at once there came an almighty
explosion from the treehouse.

A shower of leaves fell from the tree.

Polly's ladder rattled and swayed…

"Help!" she yelled. "Help!"

Yuck popped his head out of the door.

"Mind you don't fall," he said.

Polly clung to the ladder as it shuddered.

Yuck scrambled down the rope ladder and raced to find the others.

"What on earth's going on?" Mum cried, running down the garden.

"Nothing," Yuck said.

"What was that noise? And what are you doing on Dad's ladder, Polly?"

"Yuck's been doing something bad in the treehouse!" Polly said.

Mum raced to the ladder.

"Come down."

"But there's something in the treehouse, Mum!" Polly told her.

"It's all right dear, I'll have a look. You come down from that ladder, it's dangerous."

Polly stepped down to the ground.

Mum stepped onto the ladder.

"Oh no," Tom Bum whispered.

"We're done for," Fartin Martin whispered.

They watched as Mum headed up to the treehouse. "If she smells THE ROOM CLEARER there'll be no more Fart Cl— I mean no more You-Know-What," Little Eric whispered.

"If she smells THE ROOM CLEARER there'll be no more *Mum!*"

"I've got it covered," Yuck said.

Everyone watched as Mum climbed the ladder…

For a moment there was silence.

Then Mum opened the treehouse door. "There's nothing in here, Polly," she said.

"But there must be!"

Fartin Martin, Tom Bum and Little Eric looked at each other.

"Why can't she smell it?" Little Eric whispered.

"There's nothing in here except an old box," Mum said.

"That's mine!" Polly cried. "That's
my box!"

"No it isn't," Little Eric said.

Mum carried it down. "Perhaps it's time
you all came indoors."

Polly grabbed the box from Mum. "It's
mine," she repeated.

As Mum walked back up to the house,
everyone followed behind her.

"Look what I've got!" Polly said to Yuck. "Now your secret club isn't going to be so secret!"

"Give it back," Little Eric said. "It's not yours."

"It is now," Lucy told him, sticking her tongue out.

Polly and Lucy ran into the house and carried the box to Polly's room.

Fartin Martin, Tom Bum and Little Eric looked at Yuck.

Yuck was laughing.

Polly sat on her bed and put the metal box on her lap.

"Let's see what's inside," she said to Lucy.

Polly lifted the lid and…

Polly looked at Lucy.

Lucy looked at Polly.

They screamed.

Their noses curled around the sides of their faces...

A cola-coloured bubble rose from the box. Then another. And another. The bubbles burst.

**PARP! PARP! PARP!**

Polly and Lucy could hardly breathe.

**CLUCK! CLUCK! CLUCK!**

Their throats burned. They coughed and choked.

**WOOF! WOOF! WOOF!**

It was the worst smell ever!

It seeped into their hair and clung to their skin.

"PHWOARRR!"

Polly and Lucy gasped.

The box was steaming.

Something was flapping inside it.

**FLIPILLOPOLIPILLOPOL!**

They could taste the smell through their teeth.

Something crept out silently.

━━━━━━ !

"Dead rats!"

**P P P P POP POP POP POP POP POP... BANG!**

They covered their ears but there was no escape.

Gas crept along the floor and up the walls.

Their eyes started to water.

"Help!" they moaned. "Help!"

Tears were streaming down their faces.

There was a knock at the door.

"What's going on in there?"

"Help! Help!"

Mum opened the door. Yuck, Fartin Martin, Tom Bum and Little Eric were standing behind her.

Mum pinched her nose.

"Polly, Lucy — it stinks in here! Have you been farting?"

# YUCK'S SICK TRICK

Yuck opened one eye.

He looked at his clock – half-past seven.

Just two hours until school. Just two hours until the spelling test with Mrs Wagon the Dragon!

I DON'T WANT TO GO TO SCHOOL! Yuck thought.

He pulled the duvet over his head.

Yuck imagined the Dragon leaning over
his desk, her eyes black – not just black in
the middle but black around the outside
too – like deep dark holes.

"How do you spell PUNISHMENT?"
she boomed.

She poked him with her umbrella.

Yuck's stomach tightened. He hadn't learned a single word.

The Dragon pushed the tip of her umbrella up Yuck's nose and…

"It's time to get up, Yuck," Mum called.

Yuck fell out of bed onto the floor and searched for his spelling book.

He sifted through his *OINK* comics, through his pants and muddy trainers, through his water pistols and gunge balls. He brushed the dandruff and plastic spiders from his desk, then lifted the lid and picked through the slugs in Slime City. He ate through the chocolate stash hidden under his pillow. He hunted under his bed, through the mould and mushrooms of

Swampland. He searched his wardrobe –
just moths and a bag of old scabs. Then
he stood on his bed and reached up to
the dust shelf – the shelf where Yuck
collected dust.

There it was, half-buried – his spelling
book. Yuck took it down and opened it.

Stuck to the first page was half a cheese
sandwich. Yuck peeled it away and revealed
a list of words.

Library
Grammar
Responsibility
Politeness
Sensible

It's not fair – the Dragon always picks difficult words, Yuck thought.

He looked at the sandwich. A furry green mould was growing on it.

He gave it a sniff.

She never picks good words, he thought, words like YUCK or VERRUCA or VULTURE.

Yuck reached to the glass tank on his windowsill.

She never picks words like SNOT or SKIDS.

Inside the tank was his smells collection – six rotten eggs, a leaky can of fart spray, a pickled onion and a pair of smelly red socks.

Yuck held his breath and lifted the lid.

The tank belched a cloud of gas.

Yuck threw in the sandwich and slammed the lid down.

The tank rattled.

She never picks words like FUNGUS or FIB or FOOD POISONING.

Food poisoning! Yuck had an idea.

He stuffed his spelling book behind the radiator and hopped into bed, clutching his stomach.

"AAR, OOO, OWW!" he wailed.

"What's going on in there?" Polly
Princess called from the hallway.

"I'm TERRIBLY ILL," Yuck said.

His sister thumped into his room.

"Where's my pink pencil case?" she
demanded.

"Go away, Polly, I'm ill," Yuck said.

"I've got Art with Miss Fortune today and I need my pink pencil case. Where is it?"

"How should I know? My tummy hurts. My teeth are ch-ch-ch-chattering. I can't even t-t-t-talk properly."

"Stop pretending," Polly said.

"AAR, OOO, OWW! I'm not."

"Yes you are. You've got a spelling test with the Dragon today, haven't you?"

Yuck placed the pillow over his head.

"Go away, Polly. You're making my ears hurt."

"I bet you haven't learned your words," Polly said.

"OWWWW!" Yuck wailed. "I'm ill. I can't go to school."

Polly stomped down the stairs. "Mum!" she cried. "Yuck won't give me my pink pencil case!"

When she was gone, Yuck leaned over the side of his bed and peered underneath.

There, in the middle of Swampland, was Polly's pink pencil case, full of ketchup.

Floating face down in the ketchup was Bonypart, Yuck's glow-in-the-dark skeleton.

"Yuck, it's time to get ready for school!"
Mum called.

The pencil case was Bonypart's blood-bath. No way could Polly have it back.

Yuck heard footsteps.

He rolled and twisted, yowling and howling, wheezing and wailing.

Mum came in with Polly behind her.

"Yuck, have you seen Polly's pencil case?"

"Did someone say something? I can't hear. I've got earache," Yuck moaned.

"I said WOULD YOU LIKE SOME CHOCOLATE?"

Yuck peered out from beneath his duvet. "Chocolate! Yes please, Mum!"

"Well tough, I haven't got any. Now get up and give Polly her pencil case. You're both going to be late for school."

"I haven't got it."

"Liar!" Polly said.

"Double liar. No return."

Polly stuck out her tongue. "I'll get you back," she said. "You wait."

Yuck gulped and gasped and groaned.

"OHHHHHHHH! I'm too ill to argue. I have a headache," he moaned.

Mum opened Yuck's curtains.

"DON'T! I'll go BLIND!"

Yuck scrunched his eyes.

"It's disgusting in here, Yuck. Why haven't you cleaned your room?"

"But I like it like this, Mum. It's full of germs."

"It's gross," Polly said. Yuck rolled over.

"Oh, my head. My head hurts."

"Probably from playing computer games all evening," Mum said.

"And I've got stomach ache."

"Probably from all the ice cream you ate last night."

"And I can't move."

"YUCK! It's time to get up!"

"But I can't move. My whole body's gone numb."

"Well, you don't look ill to me," Mum said.

She whipped back his duvet.

"Don't get too close! I might be sick!"

"Get out of bed, Yuck! And put on some clean pants! You've been wearing those for a week!"

Polly pinched her nose.

"But they're my favourite pants, Mum." Yuck scratched his bottom.

"I thought you couldn't move," Polly said.

"Skids!" Yuck swore.

Yuck decided that when he was
EMPEROR OF EVERYTHING, he'd
order a huge pink pencil case to be made –
sister-sized. Then he'd fill it with cold sick,
push Polly in and zip it up – for ever.

"By the time I count to ten I want you
washed, dressed and at the breakfast table,"
Mum said.

"But I feel sick."

"One… two… three…"

Mum and Polly went downstairs.

Yuck lay in his bed, groaning.

"… four… five… six…"

BUT I DON'T WANT TO GO TO SCHOOL!

"… seven… eight… nine…"

Yuck jumped out of bed and opened the lid of his desk. He took a slug from Slime City and wiped it round his  nose. The slug slime dripped like snot as if he had a cold.

He opened his wardrobe and took out his bag of scabs. He grabbed a handful, licked them and stuck them to his face.

"… nine and a half…"

Yuck whipped his clothes on and hurtled
into the kitchen.

"What on earth do you look like?" Polly
said.

"I think I've got a disease!"

"Then wash your hands," Mum said.

Yuck went to the sink, turned on the tap
and squeezed some washing-up liquid onto
his hands.

Beside the sink he spied the leftovers

from yesterday's dinner. Half a saucepan
of spaghetti and tomato sauce. A plate
with baked beans and a fried egg in a
puddle of yellow yolk. Cold custard and
a bowl of apple crumble and melted
ice cream.

Yuck looked round to check that no one
was looking. Mum, Dad and Polly were
eating their porridge.

Yuck grabbed a handful of cold spaghetti

and picked the skin off the leftover custard.
He scooped up some apple crumble and ice
cream, and scraped the egg and baked
beans from the plate. He mixed and
mashed everything together with his fingers,
squishing and squidging, squeezing and
squirting, squashing and sloshing!

It felt slippy and sloppy and wet and
lumpy – just like sick.

He stuffed the mush into his trouser pockets.

"All clean," he said, his pockets squelching as he sat down and helped himself to a big bowl of Monster Snaps.

"I hope these do the trick!"

"What are you talking about, Yuck?" Dad asked.

"I hope these Monster Snaps make me better," Yuck told him.

"Monster Snaps won't do you any good," Polly said. "They're full of sugar and colourings."

Yuck reached for the milk and pushed it over, splashing it onto Polly's lap.

"YUCK!" Polly shrieked.

"What IS the matter with you this morning?" Dad said.

"I'm ill, Dad. My body's been taken over by a deadly disease."

"Then you should eat a healthy breakfast like Polly."

"More porridge?" Mum asked.

"Yes please," Polly said.

"Yes please," Dad said.

"Porridge is disgusting," Yuck mumbled.

Mum placed a small bowl of porridge in front of him.

"Come on, Yuck. You must try a little bit."

While everyone was eating, Yuck tipped the porridge into his trouser pockets.

"I've finished," he said.

Mum, Dad and Polly looked at Yuck's empty porridge bowl. "That was quick!"

Yuck stood up. "Can I play with Furball now?"

He walked over to Furball the cat, who was eating his breakfast by the fridge.

"Yuck! Come and sit down!"

Yuck gave Furball a stroke, then scooped up a handful of cat food.

"Good boy!" he said.

"It's rude to leave the table before everyone's finished," Mum told him.

"But I still feel ill. TERRIBLY ill... HORRIBLY ill."

Yuck stuffed a handful of soggy Monster Snaps up his nostrils.

His nose tingled.

"I've got a cold," he said.

"Atchoo!"

Monster Snaps and sneezy gunk splattered Polly's hair.

"YUCK!"

"I can't help it," he said. "Atchoo!"

The scabs on his face broke loose and flew across the table.

"YUCK!" Polly screamed. "Mum! Dad! Look what Yuck did!"

The scabs were stuck to Polly's face.

"YUCK!" Dad shouted.

"I can't help it. I'm contagious."

"You don't look ill to me," Dad said.

Yuck stirred the sick in his pockets, then wiped his hands on the tablecloth.

"You were fine yesterday," Mum said.

"Well I'm not now. I'll probably have to stay at home and watch television so no one catches it."

"This wouldn't have anything to do with Mrs Wagon's test today, would it, Yuck?" Mum asked. "Polly told me all about it."

Yuck glared at Polly.

"How do you spell BIG TROUBLE?" Polly whispered.

Yuck jumped up.

"I feel WOOZY! I feel WHEEZY! I feel QUEASY!" he said.

He threw his arms back.

"I think I'm going to faint!"

He fell to the kitchen floor like he'd been zapped by the Xarg.

"Yuck?"

THIS IS WHAT the XARG LooK LiKE

94

Yuck opened his eyes and saw Mum, Dad and Polly looking down at him.

"What test?" he asked.

"Mrs Wagon's spelling test."

"The Dragon's gonna getcha," Polly whispered.

"Is that today? I must be losing my memory, too."

Yuck turned towards Dad. He clutched his throat.

"I can't breathe," he croaked.

"You look fine to me," Dad said.

Yuck turned towards Mum. He clutched his stomach.

"I feel sick," he moaned.

"You look fine to me," Mum said.

Yuck turned towards Polly.

"What's that in your pocket?" Polly asked.

The tomato sauce from the spaghetti was oozing out of Yuck's trousers.

"I'M BLEEDING!" Yuck shrieked.

He clutched his leg.

"URGH, AAR, OOO…"

He rolled his eyes and pretended he was dying.

"He's faking it," Polly said. "He's not ill. He hasn't learned his words and he's in BIG TROUBLE."

Yuck clutched his heart.

"It's been a good life," he gasped. "I forgive you, Polly. You can have my smells collection when I'm gone."

Mum, Dad and Polly looked at each other.

"Yuck never lets me near his smells collection," Polly said suspiciously.

Mum scratched her head.

Dad scratched his head.

Yuck lay completely still.

For the first time all morning, Mum and Dad looked concerned.

"Can Polly have your fart spray?" Mum asked.

"Yes," Yuck said.

"Can Polly have your rotten eggs?" Dad asked.

"Yes," Yuck said.

Dad looked at Mum.

Mum looked at Dad.

They both looked at Polly.

"Can I have your… smelly socks?" Polly asked.

Yuck gulped. He thought of Polly washing his smelly socks and spraying them with perfume. Then he thought of the spelling test and the Dragon dragging him to the front of the class.

"Only if I DIE," Yuck said.

He closed his eyes.

"He might be…"

"He could be…"

"He's not!" Polly said. "He's not ill!"

"Perhaps I'd better fetch the thermometer, just in case," Mum said.

Yuck jumped up. "And perhaps I'd better go back to bed, just in case!"

He ran out of the kitchen and through the hallway.

He reached into his pockets, scooped out
two handfuls of mushy sick and threw them
against the walls.

SPLAT!

Apple porridge stuck to the mirror.

Spaghetti crumble slid down the
wallpaper.

He ran up the stairs, scooped out two

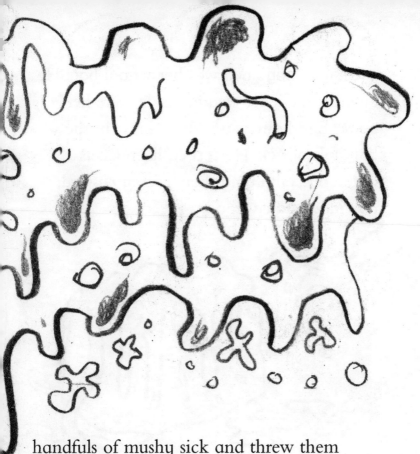

handfuls of mushy sick and threw them
against the ceiling.

SPLAT!

Eggy ice cream covered the light bulb.

Fried custard dripped onto the stairs.

He scooped out two handfuls of mushy
sick and...

Polly's bedroom door was wide open.

Yuck tiptoed inside.

Beside Polly's bed was her school bag. He opened it. Packed neatly inside were her books and homework. Yuck threw in the handfuls of sick. He turned his pockets inside out, emptying them – cold custard, porridge and cat food.

Then he closed the bag, giggled and ran to his room.

Dabbing his mouth with his sicky fingers, he dived under his duvet.

Mum came in.

"I've been sick, Mum," Yuck spluttered. "It was horrible. It poured out – everywhere!"

"I think I may have trodden in it," Mum said, looking at her shoe.

It was covered in sick, right up to her ankle.

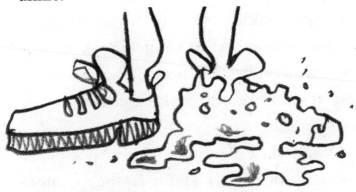

She poked the thermometer into Yuck's sicky mouth. "Keep that there."

Yuck took it out.

"I've been thinking. Perhaps Polly's pencil case is under the sofa," he said. "She always does her drawing in the sitting room. Why don't you look?"

"You must be REALLY sick, Yuck. First your smells collection, now Polly's pencil case. It's not like you to think about your sister."

Mum poked the thermometer back in. But as she left, Yuck laid it on the radiator. Then he reached under the bed and dipped his finger in Bonypart's blood-bath. He dabbed the ketchup over himself, covering his chest and legs with red spots.

When he heard Mum returning, he got under the duvet and popped the hot thermometer back in his mouth.

"Did you find Polly's pencil case?" he asked.

"She's looking now."

Mum took the thermometer out. Her eyes bulged.

"One hundred and four!" she yelled.
"Yuck, you're virtually dead!"

"I did try to tell you."

Then the door opened. It was Dad.

"I've come to see the patient."

Yuck threw off the covers and Dad and
Mum screamed.

AAAAAGGGGHHHH!!!

Polly ran up the stairs.

"What is it?" she yelled.

"SPOTS!" Mum cried.

"Chicken pox," Yuck croaked.

"He's already had chicken pox. You can't get it twice," Polly said.

"German measles," Yuck groaned.

"He's had the injection," Polly reminded them.

"French measles, then," Yuck said. "But

I'll be brave. I don't want to miss Mrs
Wagon's test."

"Hopefully, it's something really nasty,"
Polly muttered.

"Polly!" Dad said.

"Well it would serve him right for taking
my pink pencil case."

"Will you be quiet about your
pencil case, Polly! Can't you see your
brother's ill?"

"But I need it for school. I've got
Art today!"

Polly stormed out the door and went to
her room.

Rockits! Yuck thought.

He lifted one leg out of bed. "AAR,
OOO, OWW!"

"What are you doing, Yuck?" Mum
asked, tucking him back under the duvet.

"I'm going to help Polly find her pencil
case," Yuck said.

"You're not going anywhere," Mum
told him.

She looked at Dad. "I'm going to stay and look after poor Yuck. Can you walk Polly to school?"

"But the test!" Yuck croaked.

Dad went downstairs to put his coat on.

"But I can't miss the Drago— I mean Mrs Wagon's spelling test!" Yuck said.

"No buts, Yuck. You're far too ill. You're NOT going to school today!"

Yuck twanged his pants. "Oh well, if you insist, Mum."

Mum puffed up Yuck's pillows and he snuggled down, smiling.

"Can I have a glass of Coola Cola for being brave?" he asked.

"Of course," Mum said.

"And could you bring the television in so I can watch it in bed?"

"Of course," Mum said.

Yuck was feeling better already.

"Come on, Polly, you'll have to go without your pencil case," Dad called up the stairs. "We don't want you to be late for school."

Suddenly there came an almighty scream from Polly's room.

"UUURRRGGGHHH!" Polly shrieked. "Someone's been sick in my bag!"

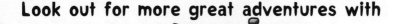